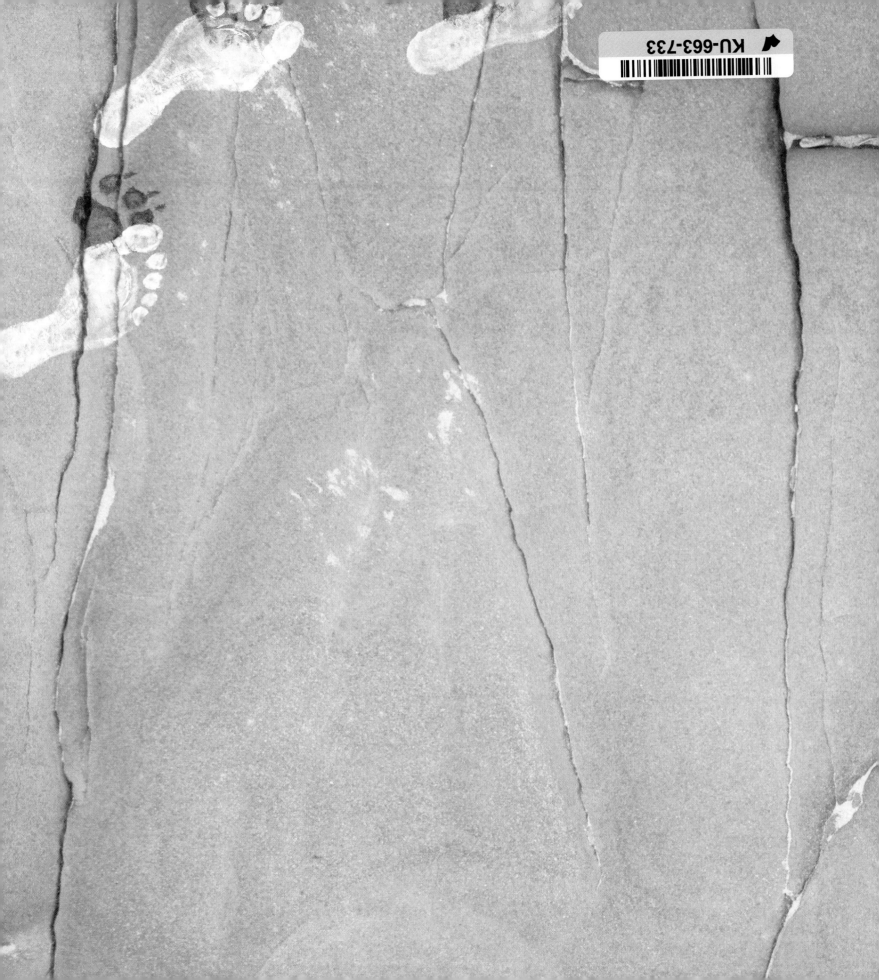

For Alicia with love from Auntie Jeannie JW

For The Siegels, The Freytags and Wild Children
everywhere! LF

First published 2012 by Walker Books Ltd, 87 Vauxhall Walk, London SE11 5HJ
This edition published 2015
2 4 6 8 10 9 7 5 3 1
Text © 2012 Jeanne Willis Photographs © 2012 Lorna Freytag
www.jeannewillis.com   www.lornafreytag.com

This book has been typeset in Tree Boxelder

Printed in China

British Library Cataloguing in Publication Data:
a catalogue record for this book is available from the British Library
ISBN 978-1-4063-5991-6
www.walker.co.uk

WALKER BOOKS
AND SUBSIDIARIES
LONDON • BOSTON • SYDNEY • AUCKLAND

This Walker book belongs to:

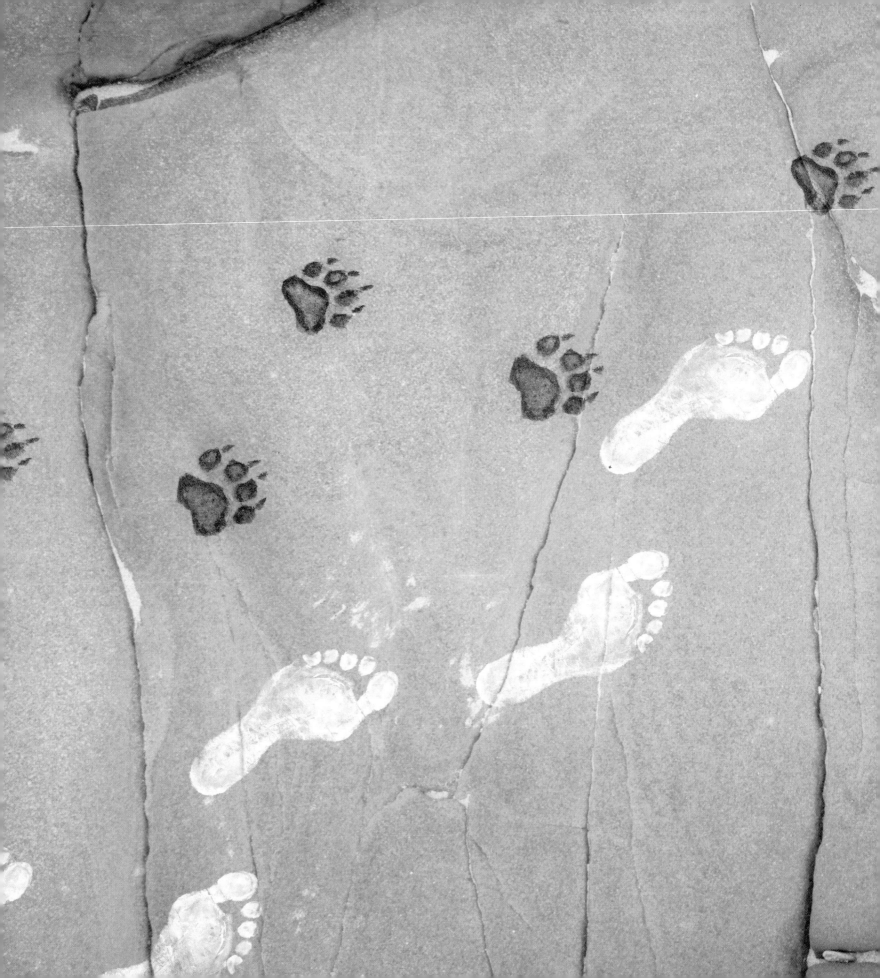

Wild Child

JEANNE WILLIS   LORNA FREYTAG

I am a child,
the very last child,
The very last child
left in the wild.

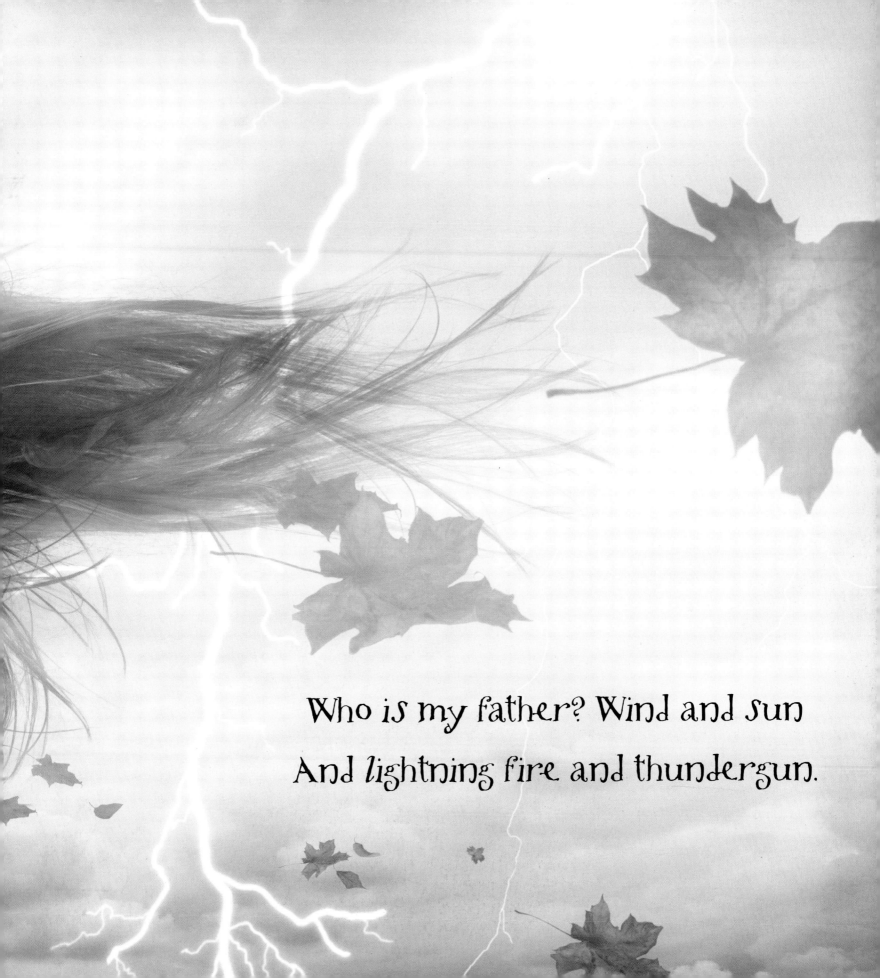

Who is my father? Wind and sun
And *lightning fire* and thundergun.

Who is my mother? Moon and sea
And stars and earth gave birth to me.

Who are my brothers? Bug and Bear
And Badger, Bat and Fox and Hare.
Who are my sisters? Deer and Mole
And Skylark, Squirrel, Vixen, Vole.

Where do I live? Wherever I wish.
I run with the rabbits, I swim with the fish.

What do I eat? Whatever tastes best
From hedgerow, field and farm and nest.
What do I drink? I drink rain by the drop,
Dew on a daisy is my fizzy pop.

Where do I go?
Wherever feels good.
The foot of the mountain,
the heart of the wood.

Why am I hiding and why must I run?
The grown-ups will catch me and ruin my fun.

They caught the wild children
and put them in zoos,
They made them do sums
and wear sensible shoes.

They put them to bed
at the wrong time of day
And made them sit still
when they wanted to play.

They scrubbed them with soap
and they made them eat peas,
They made them behave
and say pardon and please.

They took all their wisdom
and wildness away –
That's why there are none
in the forests today.

Except for just one.

How I wish there were two.

Hey, I've just seen another Wild Child...

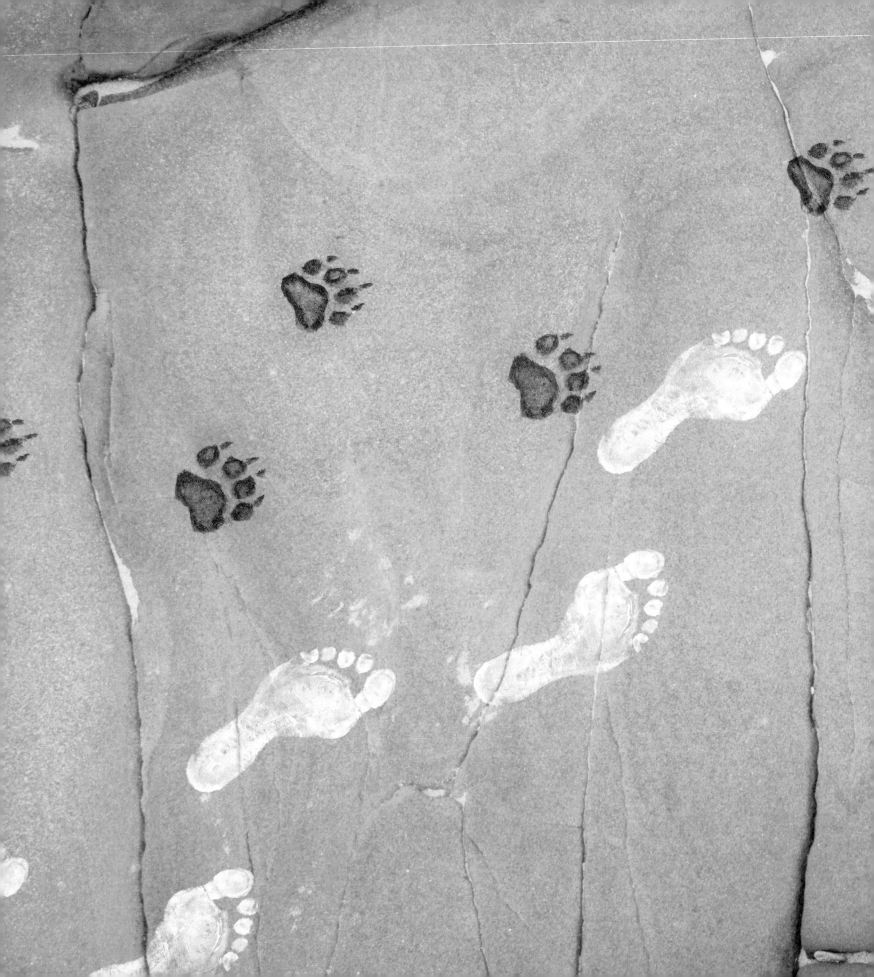

Jeanne Willis

has written over eighty picture books, poetry books, television scripts and novels for children of all ages.
Her teenage novel *Naked Without a Hat* was shortlisted for the 2003 Whitbread Children's Book Award.
Jeanne can do cartwheels and she lives in London.

Lorna Freytag

has travelled the world working as a children's photographer and, while doing so, discovering
her passion for children's literature. She has written and illustrated a number of picture books;
Wild Child was shortlisted for the 2013 Little Rebels Children's Book Award.
Lorna now lives in the west of Scotland with two of her own wild children.

By the same author:

ISBN 978-1-4063-4987-0

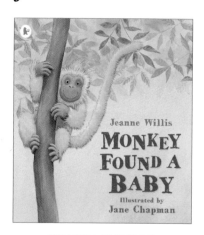

ISBN 978-1-4063-5267-2

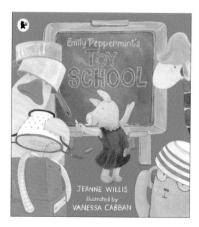

ISBN 978-1-4063-6005-9

ISBN 978-1-4063-1618-6

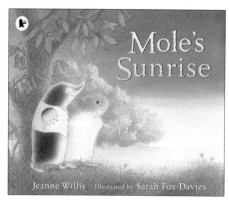

ISBN 978-1-4063-3778-5

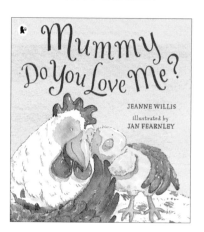

ISBN 978-1-4063-1765-7

Available from all good booksellers

www.walker.co.uk